MARVEL
SUPER HEROES COLLECTOR'S CLUB
SPIDER-MAN
AND THE MENACE of MYSTERIO
Scott Ciencin
Scholastic Inc.
New York Toronto London Auckland Sydney
Mexico City New Delhi Hong Kong Buenos Aires

Designers: Emily Muschinske, Kim Sonsky

Cover Design: Michaela Zanzani

Cover illustration by Yancey Labatt

Special thanks to Marvel: Mickey Stern, Jeff Poulin, Carl Suecoff,
James Hinton, and Matthew Primack

No part of this publication may be reproduced or stored
in a retrieval system, or transmitted in any form or by any means,
electronic, mechanical, photocopying, recording, or otherwise, without
written permission of the publisher. For information regarding permission,
write to Marvel Entertainment, Inc.
417 Fifth Avenue
New York, NY 10016

Copyright © 2006 by Marvel Entertainment, Inc.
All rights reserved.

Published by Scholastic Inc., 557 Broadway,
New York, NY 10012, by arrangement with Marvel Entertainment, Inc.
SCHOLASTIC and associated logos are trademarks and/or registered
trademarks of Scholastic Inc.

ISBN 0-439-90040-9

12 11 10 9 8 7 6 5 4 3   7 8 9 10 11/0

Printed in the U.S.A.
First Scholastic printing, October 2006

Table of Contents

 CHAPTER ONE

ommy "The Twitch" Tiarelli knelt in the shadows of the stinky alley, his lean body still clothed in his orange prison jumper. His grimy hands greedily plunged into the purse he'd stolen moments after escaping police custody. He rooted within it like a fat rat in a garbage can, his heart leaping as his fingers closed around cash and credit cards.

A breeze bristled the hairs at the nape of his neck. *A breeze? But there was no—*

Twwwwipppppp!

Tommy yelped as something fastened onto his back and hauled him high into the air. The blurring alley whirled below him. No, it wasn't whirling, *he* was!

"Okay," said a taunting voice from just above him, "give that back. Give, give…sheesh, you're worse than a Chihuahua with a chili dog!"

The world flip-flopped, and Tommy thought he might lose his lunch. Now he hung upside down, staring up into the sun. A masked face moved before the blinding light—a masked face covered in webs.

"Spider-Man!" he cried, the purse finally falling from his terror-stricken grip.

"Thanks, Tommy. I'll return that later," Spider-Man promised. "First, I'm taking you back to your buddies in blue."

Tommy yelped and twitched as Spider-Man sailed through the streets with him and delivered the wanted criminal into the waiting hands of the police.

Twenty minutes later, after returning the stolen purse, Spider-Man raised his mask and chomped

down on a hot slice of Nunzio's double-double cheese and pepperoni pizza pie.

Deee-lish!

Perched atop the twenty-seven-story Stanley office building, the spectacular Spider-Man took another bite as he looked out on to the packed streets of Manhattan.

He had already stopped three muggings and a bank robbery that day—and had the photos to prove it. By day, Spider-Man's alter ego was Peter Parker. Peter worked as a freelance photographer for the *Daily Bugle.* Sales of his pictures of Spider-Man paid for his college classes and helped his Aunt May make ends meet.

Even so, he was barely scraping by. A slice of pizza here and there was splurging!

Spider-Man opened the latest issue of the *Daily Bugle* and checked out the photo he had taken of himself fighting the Black Cat. The female thief had tried to steal an ancient Egyptian amulet worth millions from the Museum of Natural History. But he had stopped her.

"Hey, not a bad shot," he said, about to take another bite of his pie. But he froze as he read the headline:

TERRIBLE TWOSOME TERRORIZE CITY!

The article blamed the attempted robbery on Spider-Man, naming the Black Cat as his accomplice. Spider-Man shook his head. *What will it take to convince everyone that Spidey is a hero, not a menace?*

And poor Aunt May. She's probably at home right now reading and believing this stuff, even after I—after Spider-Man—rescued her from the Vulture just last week. If only I could just tell her the truth, that I am Spider-Man, I—

The familiar tingle of the hero's Spidey sense sent a shocking jolt of energy through his every nerve. Sharply casting his gaze across the rooftop and the nearby buildings, Spider-Man could see no danger.

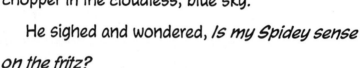

The soft, steady *whup-whup-whup* of a helicopter's blades fell to his ears and he jerked his head up to see a harmless weather service chopper in the cloudless, blue sky.

He sighed and wondered, *Is my Spidey sense on the fritz?*

Just as he was turning away, he caught something from the corner of his vision. A man leaned out of the helicopter with a rifle in his hands!

Spider-Man slapped at his neck, where he felt a sudden sting. His fingers, already growing numb, came away from his neck bearing a tranquilizer dart.

Sinking to the roof, Spider-Man saw the world turn to black as the tranquilizer knocked him out cold. 🕷

CHAPTER TWO

pider-Man was lost in darkness, his dreams a tangled web of strange sounds and feelings. He heard the hoarse, echoing shouts of men, felt the sensation of rough, strong hands hauling him into a cold metal place that trembled and quaked...

The helicopter!

Spider-Man's eyes shot open. He sat up quickly and moved his fingers over his face. He sighed with relief. The fabric of his costume swept across his fingertips. Whoever had captured him had left him masked.

Spider-Man lived with the constant worry that his secret identity might one day be revealed. If that happened, his enemies might take revenge on the people he loved, like Mary Jane and his—

"Peter! Peter, help me!" The voice was withered and frail, one that Spider-Man had known all his life.

"Aunt May!" he hollered, leaping to his feet while scanning where he'd been taken. He was in a dimly lit, almost barren room. Rows of strange, compact machinery stood pressed up against three of the walls, while a trio of unmarked doors beckoned from the fourth. A flat-screen TV monitor gently glided down from the lights near the ceiling. On the screen, Aunt May was strapped to a table. The elderly woman struggled frantically while calling Peter's name.

"Let her go!" Spider-Man demanded. "It's me you want."

An electronically altered voice murmured, "Perhaps. But I need a bit of leverage if I'm to guarantee that you do as I say. This old woman you saved from the Vulture last week should prove satisfactory. You see, she is in an isolated chamber that will be flooded with an experimental gas in exactly one hour. That gas is likely to leave her in a coma for the rest of her life. If she's lucky."

"Let..." Spider-Man almost called the woman on the screen "Aunt May" again. He had to be careful. May Parker's kidnapper had no idea that this "Peter" she was calling to was actually him. Neither did Aunt May. "Let the woman go."

Ignoring his demand, the voice continued. "There are three doors before you. Three doors, three dooms. Defeat each of them and you just may solve the riddle of this place and save the woman. Just remember, you'd better keep on top of things!"

Spider-Man saw a time counter appear on the screen next to the image of Aunt May. His aunt's life was in the hands of a madman and Spider-Man had no choice but to obey the command he'd been given…at least for now.

He chose the middle door at random, swung it open, and was blinded by the light of a blazing sun. He crossed the threshold and realized that he was, impossibly, standing knee-deep in the waters of a sweltering swamp. Alligators drifted by, their predatory eyes fixed on the intruder.

Spider-Man knew that what he was looking at couldn't possibly be real. Yet he could feel the humid press of the air and see the stagnant cypress and mangrove forests in the distance.

He was in the Florida Everglades.

Spider-Man whirled, looking for the door that had taken him here, but it had vanished.

Was that machine some kind of teleportation device? Did it punch a hole in the space-time continuum and physically send me somewhere else? Spider-Man wondered.

The tingling of his Spidey sense jolted him out of his thoughts.

Swishhhhhh!

"Yikes!" Spider-Man hollered, as a raging claw split the air near his face. He somersaulted back to take in the sight of a horrible, reptilian creature. It looked like a reptile but stood taller than a man. It wore a swirling white lab coat and pants, half-shredded by a terrible transformation.

It was the Lizard.

"You dare invade my domain?" hissed the Lizard. "For this, you will be doomed!"

"What, doomed again?" asked Spider-Man. "Sheesh, it must be Thursday. Thursdays are my usual days to be doomed!"

With a cry of rage, the Lizard attacked!

CHAPTER THREE

"Doc Connors, you've got to snap out of it!" Spider-Man pleaded, as he grappled with his foe. "Oh, and do something about that breath of yours while you're at it!"

The Lizard slapped Spider-Man with a back-hand blow that sent him tumbling through the wetlands.

"Mock me at your own peril!" warned the Lizard.

"Oh, *peril*, right," replied Spider-Man, as he sprang to his feet. "Hmmm, perils would make this Friday. Dooms on Thursday, perils on Friday. So what day is it? Hmmm...now look what you did. You got me all confused. Bad lizard. Bad, bad!"

The Lizard hesitated. "That name. Connors. Why did you call me that?"

"That's who you are. Don't you remember?" asked Spider-Man. "When you lost your arm you created a formula that would regenerate it. But the formula changed you. It turned you into—"

"Enough!" screamed the Lizard. "I'll hear no more of your lies! No more!"

The monster leaped at Spider-Man, attacking with gleaming teeth and sharpened claws. Spider-Man sprang out of the way, but the claws raked his shoulder. A sting of pain shot through him as he sailed at the Lizard, pummeling him with a series of punches that drove the villain back, but did not stop him.

"Once I rid the world of Spider-Man, all humankind will bow down and tremble before the Lizard!" the monster promised.

Spider-Man laughed. "You know, they could tremble without the bowing down."

"Bah!" cried the Lizard. "You will—"

Twwwwippppp!

"—Mrrrummh?"

Spider-Man had shot his webs right at the Lizard's big mouth, gluing the monster's powerful jaws shut. "Didn't your momma tell you it's not polite to speak with your mouth full?"

The Lizard's claws raked toward Spidey's webs but the creature wasn't fast enough. Spider-Man yanked the webs high and whirled them over his head like a lasso. The Lizard, still attached to the webs, flew through the air as if he were riding on the blades of a helicopter. With a last defiant hiss, the Lizard severed the webbing—and was flung hundreds of feet away.

"Ain't I a stinker?" Spider-Man said, as he heard a thud in the distance. He felt a sudden coolness at his back and spun to see the doorway to the lab sitting in midair.

Without hesitation, he bounded through it and once again stood in the strange lab. The image of Aunt May now showed thirty-nine minutes remaining.

"So it's a riddle I have to solve," Spider-Man called to his unseen tormentor. "How about a few clues?"

A mechanical laughter filled the room. "One is all you get!"

One? thought Spider-Man. *Where was I when that one got handed out?*

Spider-Man shrugged and sneakily slipped a Spider tracer between a pair of the strange machines.

"Can't blame a guy for asking," Spider-Man said. Then he hauled open the left door and darted through the passage into a deeper darkness—as the roar of a *train* barreled into his brain. ⊗

CHAPTER FOUR

The deafening roar of the train wasn't half as
troubling to Spider-Man as the sudden
knowledge that he was standing atop it! Spider-
Man dropped down, flattening himself against the
train's roof as he struggled to regain his bearings.
Buildings flew by and the first stars of twilight
flamed into the horizon.

From the look of these buildings, I'm in

Chicago thought Spider-Man. *But looks can be deceiving.*

He pulled out the monitor to the Spider tracer he had placed between the machines in the control room.

"Interesting," Spider-Man murmured. "The signal's so strong that the tracer might only be a block or two away. So these doors aren't really sending me across the country, like it seems."

Footsteps rang out from behind Spider-Man just as his Spidey sense tingled to warn him of

danger. He spun and took in the stalking vision of the wild-maned Kraven the Hunter.

"Kraven? Where'd you come from?" Spider-Man asked. "You weren't there a second ago!"

"The only thing that matters is that I'm here to destroy you!" bellowed Kraven.

He lunged for the super hero, his hand moving in a blur. Spider-Man gasped as he felt a burning burst in his shoulder.

He stumbled back, suddenly dizzy. *He scratched me with one of his steel claws. There must have been something on it. One of his crazy potions...*

WHOOP-sh!

The hunter's whip cracked and Spidey ducked the deadly lash—but the move cost him. He nearly fell from the speeding train!

Spider-Man shot his webbing to the train's roof and steadied himself.

"I am hunter!" Kraven bragged, as he stormed toward the dizzy and shaken hero. "I have stalked you because it is my destiny to hunt the most dangerous prey of all time!"

"So I'm ranked at number one. Nice," Spider-Man muttered. As he rose, he could feel the dizziness already fading.

None of this adds up, Spider-Man thought. *I've never shaken off the effects of one of Kraven's potions so easily. In fact, that felt more like the stuff that knocked me out on the roof, just less of it. And another thing...*

"Hey, I've heard you say all those lines before on TV interviews!" Spider-Man called over the train's roar. "So why are you repeating yourself now?"

There was no answer. Instead, a pair of adamantium tentacles smacked down on either side of the webslinger.

Spider-Man flipped backward just as Doctor Octopus bounded toward him!

"Since when did this become a tag-team deal?" asked Spider-Man. "Don't I get to call anyone for my corner?"

"No," said Doctor Otto Octavius coldly. His tentacle claws tore into the steel roof of the subway train. Spider-Man heard the screams of the passengers within. One of Doc Ock's tentacles dipped in, as if to snatch up a passenger, but Spider-Man hit the tentacle with his webbing just in time.

With a tug that sent shivers of pain down his injured shoulder, Spider-Man wrenched the tentacle away from the passengers and sent Doc Ock stumbling from the speeding train.

But the mad genius caught the ledge of a nearby building and vaulted back onto the careening train. Doc Ock struck the wallcrawler

with a steel tentacle, lifting Spider-Man from his feet. The hero recovered and landed shakily.

Behind Spider-Man, Kraven stalked closer. "I see fear in the eyes of my prey!"

Spidey spun on him and pointed at the two white ovals covering his eyes. "Really? How well are you looking at my mask, anyway?"

Despite his jokes, Spider-Man was worried. How could he defeat two of his greatest foes atop this train while keeping the people within it safe?

Answer: He couldn't.

Aiming his webshooter at a passing flagpole, Spider-Man streaked away from the train.

A tentacle suddenly smashed into Spidey's chest, driving him back against a building. Concrete burst out from either side of the webslinger, and Doc Ock's claw tightened around his chest.

POW!

The train sped away, its passengers safe.

Kraven leaped to a nearby ledge. "Let me play with him a while. I know a trick or two myself."

"Quiet, simpleton," hissed Doc Ock at his partner. "It is my intelligence, not your mere animal cunning, that has won this fight."

Suddenly, an idea gripped Spider-Man.

"Listening to Kraven here just made me think about all the times he's been on TV, doing interviews, being recognized for how great he is... I guess brains can't get you everything, right Doc?"

Uproarious laughter burst from Kraven. "The Spider has a point, scientist!"

"Does he?" asked Octavius. With a shocking suddenness, Doc Ock released Spider-Man and attacked Kraven.

"We'll see who laughs at the genius of Otto Octavius and lives!" the madman hollered.

Spider-Man clutched his aching ribs and

breathed another sigh of relief as his enemies
fought each other and left him alone.

A cool breeze swept past him and he craned his
neck to see the doorway appear in the side of the
building. He'd won!

Spider-Man darted through the door and once
again found himself in the control room. The
ticking clock beside the image of the fear-ridden
Aunt May read 19:07. Nineteen minutes left, one
door to go.

That door was where his final challenge
waited...if he kept playing the game.

Spider-Man stepped close to the computer
equipment. *What would happen if I just smashed
all this stuff, I wonder...?*

"I wouldn't," said the mechanized voice, as if

whoever was watching him had read his mind. "Attempt to destroy any of this machinery and the gas will be released instantly."

"You said there was a clue," Spider-Man growled. "What clue?"

"Merely that you must keep on top of things, remember?"

This time, he did remember. He thought that had been a taunt. Instead, it clearly meant something. *But what?* He needed time to think. But if he hesitated any longer to reason out the riddle, the madman might release the gas on Aunt May!

Taking another look at the clock, Spider-Man walked through the final door.

A dark, cloudy night greeted him as he stepped out onto the streets of Manhattan. His Spidey sense flaring, the wallcrawler suddenly spotted Electro, the master of electricity. "Oh, so now I've got to deal with you," Spider-Man called. "Yikes!"

"Aren't you going to say it's *shocking*?" asked Electro with his typical insane glee.

"Uh-uh. If I went for one that obvious, I'd lose my wisecracking license!"

Electro raised his hands and pointed at a boy and girl quaking in fear halfway down the street.

Those kids are in danger. No time for kidding around. I've got to save them!

Spider-Man leaped into action, snatching up the children just as a burst of electricity snaked across the street tossing several cars at them. Spider-Man set the kids down and looked over his shoulder. Electro was still there, lightning crackling around his hands. Spider-Man quickly cast his gaze to where he'd dropped off the kids and was surprised to see that they had vanished.

"Hey, where did they..."

The hero's Spidey sense tingled again and he quickly looked up into the sky.

"Did you miss me, webslinger?" asked the soaring Green Goblin, as he launched one of his fiery pumpkin bombs at the hero.

Spidey easily dodged the attack.

"Come on, Gobby—how can I miss you if you won't go *away*?" asked Spider-Man.

Nearby, a patch of shadows rose up and took the form of Venom, really Eddie Brock who wore the black Spidey-suit that turned out to be a living alien symbiont!

"Spider-Man," cried Venom. "For so long have I waited to take my vengeance against you for rejecting me. I—"

"Yeah, you just stay there and keep talking," Spider-Man quipped. "I'll get to you in a minute!"

Woo-hoo, Spider-Man thought, as rain began to pelt down upon him. *The gang's all here!* 🕷

 CHAPTER FIVE

Spider-Man thought again about the vanished children and how so many other things just didn't add up. He decided to take a risk. As his enemies charged toward him, Spider-Man stood rock still. He didn't move a muscle. The Goblin, Electro, and Venom all stopped short, exchanging confused glances.

"But—but we're supposed to fight," Venom pleaded. "That's why we're all here. Why we exist."

"Speak for yourself," Spider-Man said. "I've got much better reasons for existing."

He looked up into the night sky and sent his webs as fast and high as they could go...which didn't turn out to be that high at all. They smacked against something thirty feet up. Spider-Man hauled as hard as he could and a chunk was torn loose. The "sky" was made of wood!

"I knew it," Spider-Man said.

He took a good look at his surroundings. *I'm on a giant stage. It's like...a movie!*

Suddenly, Spider-Man knew just who was behind all of this. He looked down at the pavement of the street and thought of the clue to the riddle—"keep on top of things."

So, you want me to stay above and not explore what lies beneath.

Spider-Man began kicking at the pavement. It quickly splintered and cracked, revealing lights and more equipment down below.

"No!" cried Venom. "You mustn't go down there!"

Enraged, the villain launched himself at Spider-Man.

The webcrawler hit him with all the strength he possessed and Venom's head popped off of his body!

"I think I knocked his block off!" Spider-Man said, glancing down at the *robot* he had just clobbered.

It hadn't just been Kraven who was saying lines from previous battles. The Lizard, Electro, Goblin, and all the rest had been doing it, too. Someone had taped his battles with these villains and programmed those lines into these mechanical duplicates!

"But—but—" sputtered the Electro robot. This does not compute! We're supposed to battle!"

"You can take up knitting instead," Spider-Man said, as he kicked in more pavement. "I hear it's pretty relaxing!"

With that, he dove into the hole he'd made.

CHAPTER SIX

Down below, Spider-Man found another computer lab much like the one in which he'd awakened. Only this one had a glass door that led to the chamber where Aunt May was being held. He saw her now, a single tear running down her cheek.

Furious, Spider-Man tore the glass door from its fittings and cast it aside. He stormed inside and saw Aunt May stiffen in even greater terror at the sight of him.

"Come on, Mrs. Parker, you know I'm one of the good guys, don't you?" Spider-Man asked gently, as he ripped away the straps binding the old woman. "Remember last week with the Vulture? How I saved you?"

"But the *Bugle* says you're a criminal, just like that Black Cat!"

"You can't believe everything you read," Spider-Man told her. "Now don't you worry, Aunt—uh, Mrs. Parker. I'll get you out of here safe and sound."

Near the door, a strange figure cleared his throat. "You shouldn't make promises you can't keep."

A man wearing an emerald costume with a large, helmet over his head stood in the doorway.

"Mysterio!" cried the webslinger.

Mysterio laughed. "Honestly, Spider-Man, I'm a bit disappointed. I expected you to get to the *bottom* of things sooner!"

"That's me, slow on the uptake," Spider-Man said. "But look out for my fastball special—courtesy of my wacky webs!"

His webs shot out and soared right *through* Mysterio. He hadn't been there at all! The figure was simply another illusion.

How am I supposed to fight what I can't touch?

Spider-Man cautiously led Aunt May out of the containment chamber and up onto the street "set." She gasped at the sight of Venom and the other two baddies, but they were frozen solid.

"That...that man Mysterio created all this?" asked Aunt May.

"Yep," said Spider-Man. "We'll probably get some big, long speech about why before too long."

Mysterio had once been a Hollywood stunt man and special effects genius. He first tangled with the webbed wonder after using his devices to copy Spidey's powers and frame him for a series of robberies. They had been bitter enemies ever since.

A thick mist suddenly rolled in from every direction at once. The hero's Spidey sense tingled.

He shot his webbing onto a building's balcony and leaped high with the startled Aunt May. He gently set her down on the balcony and said, "You'll be safe here."

"What about you?" she asked.

"Probably not," he said with a laugh. Then he flung himself down at the waiting figure of Mysterio, whom he spied only in a brief glimpse through the rolling mists.

"So what gives, Mysty?" asked Spider-Man. "Were the other villains mean to you at playtime? Is that why you created your own playground?"

"Your childish taunts have never interested me," Mysterio said from within the rolling clouds of mist. "I am your superior in every way."

"Pretty brave words for

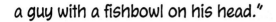

a guy with a fishbowl on his head."

Spider-Man nearly had a fix on Mysterio. He was certain he could locate the villain if he could get him to speak again...

Instead, the hero reeled under a series of blows that his Spidey sense did not warn him about. He recovered quickly and prepared for a counter-attack.

But Mysterio vanished again.

"Oh, come on, you're not using that old jammer to mess up my Spidey sense are you?" asked the wallcrawler. "You used that the first time we fought. Time to jazz up the old act, pal!"

Mysterio didn't reply.

"Why don't you fight me like one of the big boys?" taunted Spider-Man. "Or are you too much of a scaredy-pants?"

Spider-Man waited. *Hmmm. That usually gets the bad guys rushing at me all fists and glass chins. What gives?*

Suddenly, he thought of Aunt May. Leaping from the mist, he looked to the balcony and saw that she was gone.

"This has gone far enough, Mysterio!" called Spider-Man. "If you hurt her—"

"But that was my plan all along," Mysterio called from the balcony above. "I know you to be the type that would be paralyzed by guilt. If this old woman ended up in a coma because of your failure, the crushing guilt would be enough to make you give up being a hero forever. And perhaps that will still—"

Aunt May rushed out from the darkness behind Mysterio and kicked the surprised villain in the shins!

"Wha—owwww!" he hollered, falling over the railing and landing two dozen feet below.

"Frail old lady?" she called. "Hmmph!"

Spider-Man beamed with pride. "Thanks for

setting him up for me, Aunt May. Now it's
my turn!"

Spider-Man rocketed toward Mysterio,
expecting an easy victory. But the villain tapped
a section of his costume near his heart and then
leveled the wallcrawler with a powerful punch.

"I've woven micro-circuitry into my costume to
enhance my strength, making me more than a
match for you!" Mysterio boasted. He grabbed
Spider-Man by the chest,
and smacked his
domed forehead
against Spidey's skull.

CRAAACK!

Spider-Man staggered and hit the ground.

Mysterio pressed his
attack, sending a series of
flying high-kicks and
uppercuts against the hero.

Spider-Man fought back,
pounding and pummeling

Mysterio until he felt himself tiring.

Got to end this! Spider-Man realized. Then he recalled the way Mysterio had tapped that patch of costume near his chest. *That must have been how he turned on the micro-circuitry that gave him his super-strength!*

Spider-Man feinted twice, allowing Mysterio to close in on him, then he tapped Mysterio's chest in exactly the right spot. The villain gasped, his shoulders slumping.

"No, my power!" Mysterio cried.

Spider-Man brought his fist back. "Say good night, Mysty!"

The blow that knocked Mysterio out echoed for a long time through the darkened stage set.

"I must get home to check on my nephew," Aunt May said, as Spider-Man led her onto the bustling streets of Manhattan. "He's a frail boy and he tires so easily..."

Spider-Man hailed her a cab. On the top of the approaching vehicle was an ad for the *Daily Bugle*. Spidey saw his own face beneath the words:

HERO OR MENACE?

The hero sighed and tossed his last couple of bucks at the cab driver.

"I'm sure your nephew is just fine," Spider-Man said, as he waved good-bye to Aunt May.

He made a call to the police, letting them know where they could find Mysterio, then whirled as someone called his name.

"Spidey!" cried Nunzio, pizza-master supreme. "You want another slice, buddy? You look like you've had a rough day."

Spider-Man patted his hips, where his pockets would be. "Sorry, Nunzio, I'm tapped out!"

"Bah!" Nunzio said, waving his hands and calling the webcrawler over. "Two slices of double-double cheese and pepperoni, just the way you like it. On the house!"

"I guess not everybody listens to the *Bugle*, huh?" said Spider-Man.

"Just keep up the good work, Spidey. You're our hero!"

Spider-Man took the slices gracefully and shot his webs high. In seconds he was swinging between the buildings of the city. Life was good. No, better than good. It was great! With a whoop of delight, Spider-Man webbed his way out of sight. 🕷